A Note to Parents and Teachers

Kids can imagine, kids can laugh and kids can learn to read with this exciting new series of first readers. Each book in the Kids Can Read series has been especially written, illustrated and designed for beginning readers. Funny, easy-to-read stories, appealing characters and topics, and engaging illustrations make for books that kids will want to read over and over again.

To make selecting a book easy for kids, parents and teachers, the Kids Can Read series offers three levels based on different reading abilities:

Level 1: Kids Can Start to Read

Short stories, simple sentences, easy vocabulary, lots of repetition and visual clues for kids just beginning to read.

Level 2: Kids Can Read with Help

Longer stories, varied sentences, increased vocabulary, some repetition and visual clues for kids who have some reading skills, but may need a little help.

Level 3: Kids Can Read Alone

More challenging topics, more complex sentences, advanced vocabulary, language play, minimal repetition and visual clues for kids who are reading by themselves.

With the Kids Can Read series, kids can enter a new and exciting world of reading!

Pup and Hound Hatch an Egg

For Tannin and Tyler, egg hatchers eggs-traordinaire! — S.H.

For those who might eggs-pect me to dedicate a book to them — L.H.

Kids Can Press acknowledges the financial support of the Government of Ontario, through the Ontario Media Development Corporation's Ontario Book Initiative; the Ontario Arts Council; the Canada Council for the Arts; and the Government of Canada, through the BPIDP, for our publishing activity.

Published in Canada by
Kids Can Press Ltd.
29 Birch Avenue
Toronto, ON M4V 1E2

Published in the U.S. by
Kids Can Press Ltd.
2250 Military Road
Tonawanda, NY 14150

www.kidscanpress.com

The artwork in this book was rendered in pencil crayons on sienna colored pastel paper.
The text is set in Bookman.

Series editor: Tara Walker
Edited by Yvette Ghione
Printed and bound in Singapore

The hardcover edition of this book is smyth sewn casebound.
The paperback edition of this book is limp sewn with a drawn-on cover.

CM 07 0 9 8 7 6 5 4 3 2 1
CM PA 07 0 9 8 7 6 5 4 3 2 1

Library and Archives Canada Cataloguing in Publication

Hood, Susan
Pup and hound hatch an egg / Susan Hood ; illustrated by Linda Hendry.

(Kids Can read)
ISBN-13: 978-1-55337-974-4 (bound) ISBN-13: 978-1-55337-975-1 (pbk.)
ISBN-10: 1-55337-974-8 (bound) ISBN-10: 1-55337-975-6 (pbk.)

1. Dogs — Juvenile fiction. I. Hendry, Linda II. Title. III. Series: Kids Can read (Toronto, Ont.)

PZ7.H758Puh 2007 j813'.54 C2006-902913-X

Kids Can Press is a Corus™ Entertainment company

Pup and Hound Hatch an Egg

Written by Susan Hood

Illustrated by Linda Hendry

Kids Can Press

What was that?

"Oink-oink! Moo! Neigh!"

What was the fuss?

Oh, look! A birthday!

A new baby filly
stood in the straw —
the wobbliest baby
Pup ever saw!

That spring, more babies

were born each week.

Baby songs rang out:

"Mew!"

"Baa!"

"Peep!"

"Squeak!"

Pup wanted to play.
The mothers said no.
Their babies were little
and needed to grow.

Pup went to the woods
with a hangdog pout.
Hound licked his fur
and kissed his snout.

Pup sat in the grass.

And there by his leg,

he found something round.

Pup found an egg!

Hound knew what to do.

Off to the lake!

Pup rolled the egg gently

so it wouldn't break.

They took it to Duck.

She cried, “Quack! Quack!”

That egg wasn’t hers,

so Pup took it back.

Pup pushed the egg

past the pig's pen.

They went up the hill

to old Mother Hen.

But Mother Hen cried,
“Cluck-cluck! Bawk-bawk!”
That egg wasn’t hers,
she said with a squawk!

Mother Hen was busy.

She had hatching to do!

She climbed on her nest

and told them to shoo!

Pup rolled the egg

past bales of hay.

Then suddenly,

that egg got away!

Over the hilltop,
over the knoll,
the egg began
to roll and roll!

It rolled down ...

and down ...

faster and faster!

Oh, no! Watch out!

What a disaster!

The egg hit a bump
and flew high in the air.
Ducks, chicks and donkeys
all stopped to stare.

They'd never seen

an egg fly — not ever!

Birds flew, but eggs?

How strange! How clever!

Down, down it came

past a panicky jay ...

and thump!

It landed right in the hay.

“Woof!” Pup was glad.

And so was Hound!

They hugged their egg.

They snuggled around.

The egg made a noise.

The dogs jumped back.

The shell broke in two

with a crickety-crack!

It didn't quack

and it didn't cluck.

It wasn't a chick.

And it wasn't a duck.

It made no sound.

It sat blinking its eyes.

It was a turtle!

Surprise! Surprise!

Friends wanted to play.

Pup and Hound said no.

Their turtle was little

and needed to grow.

They watched him and worried
as good parents do.

Now where Pup and Hound go,

Turtle goes, too!